Dear Parent:
Your child's love of reading starts here!

Every child learns to read in a different way and at his or her own speed. Some go back and forth between reading levels and read favorite books again and again. Others read through each level in order. You can help your young reader improve and become more confident by encouraging his or her own interests and abilities. From books your child reads with you to the first books he or she reads alone, there are I Can Read Books for every stage of reading:

SHARED READING
Basic language, word repetition, and whimsical illustrations, ideal for sharing with your emergent reader

BEGINNING READING
Short sentences, familiar words, and simple concepts for children eager to read on their own

READING WITH HELP
Engaging stories, longer sentences, and language play for developing readers

READING ALONE
Complex plots, challenging vocabulary, and high-interest topics for the independent reader

ADVANCED READING
Short paragraphs, chapters, and exciting themes for the perfect bridge to chapter books

I Can Read Books have introduced children to the joy of reading since 1957. Featuring award-winning authors and illustrators and a fabulous cast of beloved characters, I Can Read Books set the standard for beginning readers.

A lifetime of discovery begins with the magical words **"I Can Read!"**

Visit www.icanread.com for
on enriching your child's readi

I Can Read! Reading 2 WITH HELP

Gilbert, the Surfer Dude

by Diane deGroat

HARPER
An Imprint of HarperCollinsPublishers

To Rosemary Brosnan

Library of Congress Cataloging-in-Publication Data
deGroat, Diane
    Gilbert, the surfer dude / by Diane deGroat.—1st ed.
        p.   cm.—(An I can read book)
    Summary: Gilbert the opossum imagines himself as Surfer Dude on a fun-filled day at the beach.
    ISBN 978-0-06-125211-2 (trade bdg.) — ISBN 978-0-06-125213-6 (pbk.)
    [1. Beaches—Fiction.   2. Surfing—Fiction.   3. Opossums—Fiction.]   I. deGroat, Diane.   II. Title.   III. Series.
PZ7.D3639 Gi 2009   2008020222
[E] 22   CIP
                                                     AC

10 11 12 13 14 SCP 10 9 8 7 6 5 4 ❖   First Edition

Contents

Chapter 1: Did I Forget Something?

It was beach day!

Father drove,

Mother read the map,

Lola looked at a book,

and Gilbert scratched his head.

"I think I forgot something,"
he said.

Gilbert tried to remember

all the things he had packed.

His boogie board was in the trunk.

His flippers and goggles were

on the floor.

He had paddles and balls,

a shovel and pail, a book and a hat.

But something was missing.

"I know I forgot something," he said.

"I'm really upset."

"I'm upset too," Lola cried.

She held up her book and said,

"There are sharks and jellyfish

and all kinds of scary things

in the water.

I am not going swimming!"

11

Mother said, "But you have a
brand-new bathing suit, Lola.
I think you will want
to go swimming."

Then Gilbert remembered

what he forgot.

"Uh-oh," he said.

"My bathing suit!"

13

Chapter 2: The Wave

At the beach, Gilbert found

a suit that said "Surfer Dude" on it.

"I think it is too big," Mother said.

"This is the one I want,"

Gilbert said.

When he put it on, he wasn't

just a possum anymore.

He was Surfer Dude!

Father laid a blanket on the sand.

Mother put up the umbrella.

Lola cried, "I'm still not going

in the water."

"You can play in the sand,"

Gilbert said.

"I'm going surfing."

"Wait!" Lola said.

"First help me dig a hole."

Gilbert helped Lola dig a deep hole.

"Okay," Gilbert said.

"I'm going in the water now."

"Wait!" Lola said.

"Help me fill my pool."

Gilbert helped Lola fill the hole
with water.

Then he picked up his boogie board
and ran to the waves.

"Here comes Surfer Dude," he said.

But a big wave knocked
Surfer Dude down.
Water got in his eyes.
Sand got in his suit.

And his boogie board went
surfing without him.

Gilbert was not a Surfer Dude.

He was just a wet possum

in a big blue bathing suit!

Chapter 3: The Scary Thing in the Water

Father said, "It looks like
Surfer Dude needs a hand."
He helped Gilbert out
to the deep water.

When a big wave came,

Father pushed the board.

Gilbert held on tight.

He was riding the wave!

He was Surfer Dude!

Then Surfer Dude felt like
something was missing.
"Uh-oh," Gilbert said.
"My bathing suit!"

Suddenly a lady yelled,

"There's something in the water!"

"I think it's a jellyfish!"

a boy cried.

"Maybe it's a shark!"

a girl screamed.

And then Gilbert saw the scary thing.

It was swimming right next to him!

Gilbert was about to jump
out of the water with nothing on!
But then he saw that the scary thing
was bright blue and had the words
"Surfer Dude" on it.
Gilbert grabbed it
before it could float away.

Everyone was looking at Gilbert.

He put the suit on and waved.

"False alarm," the lifeguard said.

"Nothing to be afraid of."

Back on the beach, Lola asked,

"Were you afraid?"

Gilbert said, "Not Surfer Dude!"

Then he said, "Come on, Lola.

Let's go in the water."

And they did.